TRIANGLE CHOKE

THE DOJO

TRIANGLE CHOKE

BY PATRICK JONES

darby creek
MINNEAPOLIS

Darby Creek
A division of Lerner Publishing Group, Inc.
241 First Avenue North
Minneapolis, MN 55401 U.S.A.

Website address: www.lernerbooks.com

The images in this book are used with the permission of: © Daniel Dempster Photography/Alamy (fighter); © iStockphoto.com/Tim Messick (metal texture); © iStockphoto.com/Erkki Makkonen (metal wires); © iStockphoto.com/TommL (punching fist), © iStockphoto.com/dem10 (barbed wire).

Library of Congress Cataloging-in-Publication Data

Jones, Patrick, 1961–
    Triangle choke / by Patrick Jones.
        pages   cm. — (The dojo)
    ISBN 978–1–4677–0630–8 (lib. bdg. : alk. paper)
    ISBN 978–1–4677–1631–4 (eBook)
    [1. Mixed martial arts—Fiction. 2. Fathers and sons—Fiction.
3. Alcoholism—Fiction. 4. Hispanic Americans—Fiction.] I. Title.
PZ7.J7242Tr 2013
[Fic]—dc23   2012037204

Manufactured in the United States of America
1 – SB – 7/15/13

WELCOME TO

If you're already a fan of mixed martial arts, in particular the Ultimate Fighting Championship (UFC), then you're probably familiar with moves like triangle choke, spinning heel kick, and Kimura. If not, check out the MMA terms and weight classes in the back of the book. You can also go online for videos of famous fights and training videos. Amateur fights are similar to the pros but require more protection for the fighters. While there are unified rules, each state allows for variation.

WELCOME TO THE DOJO.
STEP INSIDE.

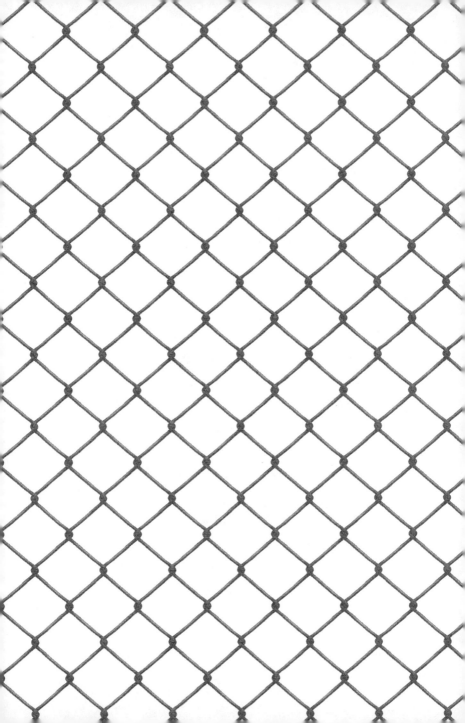

CHAPTER 1
TWO YEARS AGO

"It's a human cockfight. I won't allow you to partici-
pate, Hector," Mom yells.

I just smile. "Mom, it's not like that. Have you
even seen a mixed martial arts fight?" I know from
years of watching MMA that you need good counters. He shoots, you sprawl. He mounts, you guard.
Mom yells, I smile and ask polite questions.

"I know what two people fighting in a cage is
like. Do you think that makes you a man?"

"No, it makes me a fighter." I know how to box
and wrestle, but being a mixed martial artist is my
goal. Today's the day I asked my parents to let me

attend a new teen MMA program. I knew Mom would object. My hope is Dad will come to my rescue. He can't let me down this time.

"Hector, you're only fifteen!" she shouts, even though I'm just across the kitchen table from her. She turns toward the living room, where Dad's on the sofa with a Tecate in his left hand and the remote in his right. "Victor, didn't I tell you that if you taught him to box, he'd develop a love of fighting? Answer me!" He responds by turning up the volume of the soccer game on Telemundo and mumbling something in Spanish.

"You need to concentrate on school, on getting your grades up, on getting through your sophomore year," Mom says. It's another one of her speeches. She's got about fifteen on her playlist, and she just hit Shuffle.

"Why? So I can go to college in three years? Who is going to pay for that? You know I'm not smart enough to get a scholarship like Angelina or Eva."

"Well, we certainly won't pay for you to learn how to fight in a cage."

"I'll pay for it!" I shout. "I'll get a job. I'll clean toilets, whatever it takes for me to—"

"That's enough!" Dad shouts over the TV.

Mom and I glare at each other like two fighters might stare at the ref after a close bout. Except that, in MMA, there are three judges with scorecards. Here there's just one judge: Dad.

He mutes the TV and swallows the remaining drops of his first (but certainly not his last) beer of the evening. He walks, head down, into the kitchen, almost like the Golden Gloves champ that he was at my age. When I started training with him, he said boxing would teach me how to defend myself and teach me about life. He also said he'd never let me down. Here's his chance.

"You're not cleaning toilets," Dad growls. "I'll talk to Mr. Torrez about you working in the garage on weekends. It's time you learn a real-world skill anyway."

Mom stares at Dad and then looks away. "Victor, what are you doing?"

"You know how my parents squashed my dreams." Dad says as he turns toward Mom. "I was a champion. I could've gone pro. But they wouldn't allow it, so I won't allow this."

"Then it's on your head if Hector gets hurt! Can

you live with that?"

"He's not going to get hurt," Dad says. Eyes focused on me now.

"And how do you know that?" Mom asks.

Dad smiles at me, but Mom counters with a frown. "Because he's going to hurt the other guy first, right, Hector?" I smile back at him, but before I can answer, his expression changes, fast. His soft smile turns into a hard stare, his brown eyes sending me a clear message: I came through for you, so don't let me down.

"Thanks, Dad," I say, but he's not looking at me anymore. He glances at Mom, who glares back at him. We live in a small, square house, but today, we're in a triangle that seems like it's about to break apart. Dad reaches for another beer, Mom stomps away, and I sprint to my room to spread the news that I'm taking the first step to becoming a mixed martial arts champion.

⬚ ⬚ ⬚ ⬚ ⬚

Even before I post the news, I call Rosie.

"Hector, you won't let them mess up your pretty face," she says.

"Not going to happen," I reassure her. She asks lots of questions and I'm excited, full of answers. Except for boxing, watching MMA, and hanging with Eddie and the other guys, Rosie's the only other thing I'm serious about in my life. We had been friends for a long time, almost since first grade, but that changed a few months ago. I made my move, and she didn't block it.

"You'll come to all my fights, right?"

"Wherever you are, I am. I love you so much, Hector." I blush as my temperature rises.

"I love you too, Rosie," I say, amazed how fun and easy those words are to say.

⌑ ⌑ ⌑ ⌑ ⌑ ⌑

"I'm in," I text Eddie. He hates talking on the phone.

"Me2," he texts back. Eddie and I agreed that we'd both ask our parents—well, for him, his foster parents—to join the MMA dojo after the school wrestling season ended. Eddie had an okay season wrestling heavyweight on the JV team. I wasn't much better. I've watched so much UFC that I kept trying MMA moves, most of which are illegal in high school wrestling.

"Let's make a pact," I text. "We stick with this and we stick together."

"Like flies on dog crap."

Despite having a hard life, Eddie makes the best of it by always cracking jokes. He's the brother I never had, and I know he feels the same. If we weren't dudes, I'd call us BFFs. One day, Eddie and I will be the kings of MMA.

CHAPTER 2

"Jab, Hector, jab!" Jackson's encouraging me as I bounce hard strikes off the blockers.

"Watch this!" I shout as I throw an overhand left, uppercut right, and side kick.

"I can't. Your fists and feet are flying too fast."

I crack a rare, small smile and land another killer combination. After about five minutes, Mr. Hodge, our dojo master, calls for us to switch. The first punch Jackson throws almost knocks me off my feet.

His hand speed is slower than mine, but

his punches are powerful. One of his punches equals five of mine. Most of the time his punches don't connect, but when they do, watch out. Last week, he concussed one of the new kids even though we wear gloves and helmets when we spar and drill. Jackson doesn't have hands; he's got bricks with fingers.

After another five minutes, Mr. Hodge yells, "Wrestle!" We drop the blockers and wrestle. I stop about half his takedowns, which is a victory of sorts, but I only get him to the mat a few times. Every time he takes me down, I remember what Nong says. Defeat brews the tea of victory.

"New partners!" Hodge yells, and everybody switches. I end up with Nong. Nong, Jackson, and I are the best guys in the dojo. We're the oldest—along with two other seventeen-year-olds who joined recently—and we're the most experienced. We've trained together for over two years.

"Strike!" Hodge yells. We put our helmets back on and fan out over the dojo. Nong and I are a perfect match: he's strong on kicks, and

I'm strong on punches. He's a little better at the other striking arts, except Muay Thai. We train three times a week in MMA, and a fourth night we train in individual martial arts. I need to learn more Brazilian jiu-jitsu submissions from Mr. Matsuda since knockouts are hard to get in amateur MMA with the protective gear we wear.

"Watch this!" Nong shouts as he throws a spinning heel kick, his long black hair flying.

Nong lands a few more kicks, but I counter with punches. When he tries to fight in close, I clinch his head by wrapping my hands around the back of his neck and locking my fingers. Then I bring my knee up and slam it into his chin. Like everything else, our knees are padded because in a real fight, I would've knocked him out. When the whistle blows, Nong kicks the air in anger.

"Hector and Eric into the ring!" Mr. Hodge orders. We do as we're told. "Two three-minute rounds."

When it's time for a spar, two of us enter the ring while the other students—there are nine tonight—gather around Mr. Hodge. He alternates yelling instructions at us and telling the other students what we are doing right and wrong. Meghan, our best female fighter, stands next to him.

Eric's one of the new seventeen-year-olds and fights at light heavyweight, while I'm a weight class under at middleweight. I'm throwing punches too fast for him, so he tries to take the fight to the ground, but I block him. It's not much of a fight because both of us are playing safe.

"You can strike, Hector, but you can't win on that alone, can you?" Mr. Hodge yells.

With Mr. Hodge's question ringing in my ear, I answer with a hard leg kick, and Eric's left knee buckles. I snatch the leg and try to trip his right, but he fights it off and slams me to the mat. The wind's knocked out of me, but I remain calm as he tries to mount. I'm fighting him off when Mr. Hodge whistles to end the round. When I reach my corner, Mr. Hodge is in my face.

"You've got leg strength, and he's sloppy on

the mount," Mr. Hodge says. "If you get control of him from the body in open guard and his head's not moving, you know what to do, right?" I nod.

Eric and I touch gloves, and round 2 starts the same as round 1. I almost let him take me down. On top of me, his mount is sloppy, and I easily assume the defensive position of open guard. Like Mr. Hodge saw it all in a crystal ball, Eric's not moving his head, and I see daylight. I quickly wrap my right leg around the back of his head and pull him toward me. With my left leg, I press his outstretched right arm tight against his neck.

"Perfect triangle choke!" Mr. Hodge yells just as Eric taps out. Nong and Jackson applaud, but they shouldn't be happy. I've just added another hold to my arsenal against them.

After the spar, Mr. Matsuda shows me more variations of the triangle choke from every position using Eric as his dummy. MMA is like geometry; it's all about angles.

"You want the fight standing, but if it goes to the ground, this is your hold," he says.

"What if—" is as far as I get before I'm distracted by the dojo door slamming loudly.

"Hector, come here!" Dad shouts at me from across the wide open space of the gym.

It's Wednesday night. His night. He's early, but probably because he doesn't know what time it is. After he lost his job, he lost track of time. He lost Mom when the bottle won.

I take my eyes off Mr. Matsuda and look at Dad. He uses the wall for balance.

"Hector! I'm talking to you!" Dad yells as he stumbles a few steps into the gym, and I'm worried. Friends and family are not permitted inside without permission from Mr. Hodge.

"I'll be right back." I say and then sprint over to Dad. I can smell him from a distance.

"It's time to go."

"I'm not getting in the car with you when you're drunk."

"I'm not drunk!" Dad shouts. Then he starts cursing in Spanish. Even though I'm sweating, I feel frozen. I'm not sure what to do or say. Mr. Hodge walks slowly toward us. When he gets close, he gets a disgusted look on his face—the smell just hit him—but Dad keeps shouting. "I'm your father! You'll obey me, Hector!"

"Hector, a moment," Mr. Hodge says. I step away and Mr. Hodge talks with Dad. At first, there's a distance between them, but Mr. Hodge closes it. He's a lot taller than Dad. Soon his right arm is on Dad's shoulder. Dad reaches into his pocket and hands Mr. Hodge his keys.

Hodge shakes his head and walks back toward me. "Here," he says as he drops the keys to Dad's truck in my hand. "Hector, I don't want to see him in here like that again."

"Neither do I," I reply, shaking my head in a combination of shame and sadness. I stare at Dad and wonder what happened to the man I knew and the man that I wanted to be.

CHAPTER 3

"You feel that?" Mr. Hodge asks us. "Go ahead, touch it."

The cold silver steel chain link feels different than I expected. Nong, Jackson, and Meghan touch the high-quality cage as well. Mr. Hodge brought us to an amateur MMA show called Friday Night Fights. He used his connections to get us inside the eight-sided cage before the fights start in an hour. For now, the arena is empty. But in sixty minutes, some three hundred MMA fans will be cheering.

"Now, you see this?" Mr. Hodge points at

his face, his left finger over his left eyebrow. "This is what a real cage can do to your skin. Twenty years later and I still got the scar."

"Cool," Nong whispers. Mr. Hodge's shaved head is a road map of scars.

"When people think of a cage, they think the bars are like a prison cell," Mr. Hodge continues. "But it's really just like the fence you might have in your backyard."

"Tell them how you got that scar," Meghan says like she's prompting a story.

"It was my first pro fight, right here in St. Louis. My friends and family were there," Mr. Hodge says, and then goes on. I'm interested in the story, but I can't help thinking instead about my first fight in this very cage. It's ten weeks away, soon after I turn eighteen. I'm wondering if Mom or Dad will attend. I'm wondering if Eddie and Rosie will be there too.

"I would've choked him out when he dropped his head," Nong interrupts Mr. Hodge, a bad habit he hasn't corrected in two years. Nong's not known for his discipline or his modesty.

"I tried, but I was too tired and maybe too

nervous," Mr. Hodge explains. "That's why we do so much cardio and calisthenics. It is not just about being a better fighter but about being what?"

"The superior athlete," Meghan answers.

"We're against the cage. He's eating elbows and I feel confident. He drops his head. I start to lift a knee, but I pause. Instead of throwing the knee, I try a standing guillotine choke."

"Hard move, master, hard move," Nong says. Mr. Hodge shakes his head in agreement.

"Just like I've said a thousand times, you can't take time to decide. MMA isn't chess; it's combat. It must become instinct built on hours of drills. So when I hesitated, he rocked me with an uppercut and I bounced up against the cage. He pushed my face against the cage, and it ripped the skin. I pushed back and created distance. What happens when there's distance?"

"Somebody goes to sleep." Nong says and then snores loudly.

"I tapped out before he put me to sleep," Mr. Hodge says. "That's important. You need to surrender when it is time or risk a serious injury. I don't want any of you getting injured, understand?"

"If you don't want us hurt, then why are you bringing us the pain every day?" Jackson asks. "I mean, ain't nobody hurt me more than you, Hector, and Nong."

"No pain, no gain," Mr. Hodge says. "You're all better fighters because of it, right?"

Nong slams his right fist into the palm of his left, then brings down his right elbow hard into his palm. It echoes like a gunshot in the empty arena. Next, he bounces his palm off his knees and then throws his right foot out in a perfect spinning heel kick. After his performance, Nong laughs so hard that it's impossible not to join in, until Mr. Hodge shuts us down.

Mr. Hodge points at his head. "Your brain is the best weapon. We're training your brain to tell your body to do the right move at the right time. It's about instinct. That's why we drill so much. You help each other improve. None of you could improve just on your own, right?"

Jackson, Nong, and Meghan answer, but I'm focused on the cage. I touch it again. I think about my fight. I think about my life, how I have no other friends left, a girlfriend, or an intact family. This cage is hard, cold, and unforgiving. Just like I've become.

CHAPTER 4

"Hector, I want you to really concentrate on this next fight," Mr. Hodge shouts over the noise of the now full arena. While his connections got us into the cage, they didn't help with good seats. We're in the cheap seats. That fits, though. The one thing the four of us have in common—other than training at Mr. Hodge's Missouri MMA dojo—is we're not rich.

The two fighters come to the ring. Like me, they're middleweights, between 171 and 185 pounds. One's black, one's white—well, mostly green from tattoos. The black guy, Malone, is so built it's like his muscles have muscles. He looks as if he's been chiseled from dark marble, like Jackson.

"I got ten on the brother," Jackson says. We shake on it. We bet push-ups, not money.

"You always bet on the black guy," Nong says, then laughs.

"That's because they most always win," Jackson counters.

"Until they face an Asian, then we'll see," Nong says. It's an argument between them going back to our first class together. It's not about race, it's about style. Me, I'm a striker. My hands are like those racing movies: fast and furious. And before I even started training for MMA, Dad taught me footwork that every fighter in our dojo envies.

"Pay attention!" Mr. Hodge shouts. I glance at the program. Malone has six pro fights with five wins. Davidson, the other guy, is in his third fight and has yet to earn a W.

I can barely hear the ring announcer because the sound system is so bad. This small show is nothing like you see on TV. Like in every sport,

I guess you have to start at the bottom.

The bell rings and the fighters touch gloves. Malone is aggressive, while Davidson backs away. Malone throws a couple of jabs and hooks, but Davidson's reflexes are sharp. Malone tries knees and even a spinning heel kick, but nothing connects with any authority. Davidson moves like he's dancing on hot coals, and Malone can't touch him.

"Come on, let's see some action!" Meghan shouts. She starts clapping, but she's not cheerleading. She probably would've made a good cheerleader, actually, or school-sports superstar, but she'd rather fight. But inside the ring, she's as tough as any of us guys.

"Single leg, single leg," I hear Mr. Hodge mutter. He can't stop teaching, and he's right. Whenever Malone throws his right, he telegraphs it by putting his leg out front. Davidson's got to snatch it, take him down, and put the hurt on his body. That's what I'd do, what I will do soon.

Meghan keeps shouting, and pretty soon others in the crowd get restless. Mr. Hodge shakes his head in disgust. "This is MMA, not pro wrestling. It's a serious sport, not just a show."

Malone lands a high kick on Davidson's chin, which staggers him. Malone presses, but Davidson ties him up against the cage. Nothing's happening and the ref separates them.

"He'll try it again," Mr. Hodge says. Malone lands another high kick and it's a rerun.

"Now!" Mr. Hodge shouts. After a few jabs that miss, Malone goes for another high kick. Davidson ducks it as he shoots on Malone's vulnerable left leg. Malone hits the mat hard and Davidson's on top of him. He's got him in full mount. Malone tries to pass guard, but Davidson's got perfect position as a rainstorm of rights and lefts crash off Malone's face.

Meghan's cheering, while Jackson slumps in his seat when the ref stops the fight. TKO. As the ref raises Davidson's hand, I crack a smile thinking about Jackson owing me ten push-ups.

"Hector, what do you learn from that fight?" Mr. Hodge asks in his master's voice.

"Speed and smarts matter more than muscle." Mr. Hodge nods like Yoda. Right I am.

"You use your opponents' aggressiveness against him," Mr. Hodge says to us all, but he only looks at me. "The thing that makes someone strong can be their greatest weakness as well."

CHAPTER 5
TWO YEARS AGO

"Where's the cage?" I ask the tall black guy next to me. He just shrugs.

"Don't you know anything?" a voice says. I turn to see a stout Asian guy.

"About what?" I answer.

"In Missouri, you can't get into a cage until you're sixteen, even to train."

"And you can't even fight amateur until you're eighteen," a white kid chimes in.

"I won't need no cage to beat you two," the Asian guy says. The guy next to me just laughs, but I don't know what to think. Dad warned me it might be like *this.* He says the first day in anything is just like dogs meeting each other: everybody's sniffing and lifting their legs.

"Pretty tough talk from a little man," I counter.

The Asian guy laughs. "A skilled little man can beat an untrained big man. You wanna throw hands?"

"Students, face front!" A voice shouts from behind. The three of us and the other seven teenagers at the MMA dojo do as we're told. "Form a line, shortest to tallest. Now!"

"It's like the army," the guy next to me whispers.

"And no talking!" The voice grows louder as it grows closer. It's almost a growl.

Everybody shuts up when the bald, middle-aged man steps in front of us. He has a faint blond beard and is wearing a white gi with a green sash. He says nothing for a long time as he inspects us.

"Welcome to the first teen camp at the Missouri MMA dojo. I am your instructor, your master, and you are here to learn from me, understood?" The veins on his neck look like small blue snakes.

"Yes, sir!" Black guy snaps. Others say it but with less enthusiasm.

"I am Mr. Daniel Hodge, and I'm a retired MMA fighter. I have black belts in karate, jiu-jitsu, tae kwando, and judo. In high school, I was a wrestling and Golden Gloves boxing champion. In the army, I was also a wrestling and boxing champ." He stops and looks us square on. "What are your credentials?"

The Asian guy steps up first. "Nong Vang. Green belt in karate and black belt in judo. You can call me Nong, the Ninja Warrior. I was also state champ in football last year."

"Team sports don't matter here," Hodge says. "This is one-on-one combat."

Other people start listing their credentials, which are numerous and more than mine. Well, any credential is more than I got. I'm sizing everybody up, but I'm distracted. Where's Eddie? He was supposed to ride his bike over here with me, but he was late, as always. Hodge doesn't seem like a guy who's okay with anybody being late. Or overweight. Eddie's so dead.

Only the black dude and I are left to speak. I start, "My name is Hec—" But I'm cut off.

"Jackson James. The only belt I got is the one holding up my pants."

Everybody laughs, except Mr. Hodge. "Then what brings you here?"

"I'm gonna be Army Special Forces. The recruiter said MMA would help prepare me."

"He's right. I will make you more than fighters. I will make you athletes. I will—"

The door to the dojo opens, and Eddie walks in, slowly. "Sorry I'm late."

"You Eddie Garcia?"

Eddie nods. Hodge looks at me. "You're Hector Morales, right?"

"Yes, sir," I mumble.

"What are your credentials?" Mr. Hodge asks.

"I don't really have any, but my dad taught me to box. He was a champion like you."

"A striker," Mr. Hodge says and then turns toward Eddie. "You look like a wrestler."

"Heavyweight on the JV team. I was undefeated," Eddie says; he lies.

"A wrestler and a boxer," Mr. Hodge says. "Let's have them fight and see who wins, okay?"

Hodge directs us toward the mat in the center of the dojo. Is he serious? I'd read on the Internet that *the first practice was normally just a workout. Is he really going to have us fight?*

"I'd bet on the cute one," a voice shouts from behind us. A female voice.

I take my eyes off Eddie and turn around. There are three girls standing against the back wall. Like us, they're all dressed for combat. *Are they in the class with us? While I always like meeting females, I'm not sure how I'd feel about fighting them.*

"Thanks for your support!" Eddie yells. *I guess he's decided he's the cute one.*

"No talking!" Hodge shouts at Eddie.

"I like the skinny one," another girl says. Hodge glares in her direction. Two of the girls are giggling, while the third one—a tall, thin brunette—glares at them.

"Good thing Rosie's not here. That girl would have a fight on her hands," Eddie whispers. *I try not to laugh.* "Rosie would kill for you, Hector. She loves you something awful."

"This is how this sport began," Hodge says. "MMA started when people decided to test age-old questions. Who would win a fight between a wrestler and a boxer? Between a judo expert and a kickboxer?

The first fights were battles of different styles, but the sport's evolved."

"UFC 1 was in November 1993," a white guy says too loud. He's tall and skinny, but he looks soft. I should be thinking about fighting Eddie, but instead, I'm sizing up all the other competition.

"So, the question is not which is the best martial art. But what is the best mix of martial arts: striking, submission, and wrestling. This is the holy triangle of MMA," Hodge says. He never stops moving as he talks. "All of you are strong in one or two sides of the triangle, so we will build on those and improve your skills in other areas to make you a complete fighter. You will work harder than you've ever worked. You will work hard because there is no other choice if you want to become a champion. Let's get started."

CHAPTER 6

"Hector, tap," Jackson shouts at me. We're on the mat. He's locked me in a rear naked choke, his bicep and wrist starting to cut off the flow of blood to my brain. It's only a matter of time before I choose to surrender or lose consciousness.

"Tap!" Mr. Hodge screams. Him, I listen to. I pound my hand on Jackson's leg.

I feel a little dizzy as I start to stand, so Jackson reaches his hand out to help me up. "Good fight," I whisper. It's a lie—good fight for him, bad fight for me.

"Excellent execution, Jackson!" Hodge

shouts, then bows to Jackson in respect.

Jackson returns the bow and heads off the mat. I'm cringing inside, waiting for Hodge to yell at me, but instead he puts his hand lightly on my shoulder and speaks almost in a whisper. "You need a plan of attack before every fight, and then work it. Hector, what was your plan?"

I'm breathing heavy and it's hard to talk. "Knock him down and take him out."

He laughs. "That's always your plan and that's why you lost. Jackson knew what you were going to do so he could stop you. But he's also thirty pounds heavier and a lot stronger. When you get into the cage for the first time, it will be against someone your size."

"But I've beat everybody here my size," I say. Two years I've been coming to this dojo, and no middleweight has taken me out. When I lose, it's almost always to someone bigger. But I've beat bigger guys too. I've beat Jackson before, and then, of course, I beat up Eddie.

"I've come up with a solution for that," Mr. Hodge explains. "I talked with Josh, who runs a teen program at MMA Academy."

I don't react. I've heard that's where Eddie trains now. Since he left school, since he and I . . . well, I don't know much about him. The stab wound in my back is still fresh one year later.

"He's got several students like you who are only going to get better through actual contests with people their own size and skill level. So next week, he's going to bring over a few of his students and we'll have kind of a scrimmage game, understand?"

"Master Hodge, look at this!" Nong shouts. He's doing Bruce Lee moves against the punching bag: flying knees, spinning back fists, and other show-off karate moves.

"Nong, get serious!" Mr. Hodge shouts.

"I'm seriously ready to get into that cage," Nong says. His eighteenth birthday is only a few days after mine, so he'll be the second one to fight. Jackson's next and then Meghan.

"Then stop screwing around," Hodge says.

"I'm not. I'm getting ready," Nong says. "I watched Hector, and I knew what he was going to do. The only way to win in this sport is to do the unexpected. Everybody knows that you teach the ground-and-pound style, so that's what they'll be looking for. Well, I'll have a little surprise for them for sure." He throws a perfect spinning heel kick that rocks the bag.

"Let's go," Hodge says and motions for Nong to come over. "Shawn, get in here."

Shawn Hart is still a skinny white kid like the day I met him. He still knows more about the UFC than anyone. He plays sports at school, so he doesn't train full-time. He's flyweight, the smallest MMA weight class, while Nong is featherweight, still a few classes below me. Before Shawn steps on the mat, Hodge whispers something in his ear as Shawn puts on his sparring helmet. Nong puts on his helmet, straightens his gloves, and looks like a hungry wolf.

"Get it on!"

Nong rushes Shawn and starts throwing kicks, but Shawn blocks them. Nong leaps in the air with a high knee that connects against Shawn's chest. Shawn staggers back but stays standing. Nong loses his balance and hits the mat. Shawn pounces on him and gets a full mount. Shawn punches with his hands and uses his legs to control Nong. Mr. Hodge blows the whistle.

Shawn and Nong get up. Shawn smiles while Nong stares at the mat.

"Nong, someone in your weight class would have pounded you, but you grounded yourself," Hodge says. "You can't give away anything, am I right?" Nong nods in agreement.

"Like at UFC 77 when . . ." and Shawn is off and running. If his hands and feet were as fast and strong as his memory, he'd dominate this dojo. We all have our reasons for being here, but I think Shawn more than any of us, except maybe Nong, loves the sport itself.

"Everybody here," Hodge yells. We stop our drills or exercises and huddle around the mat. Times like this make MMA feel like a team sport. Not that I've ever played one.

"As you know, we have four fighters about ready to enter their first amateur competition. They'll be taking on fighters more experienced but, I guarantee you, not better trained. So to get them ready, I've lined up fights with another dojo's teen program. We'll meet at the MMA Academy next week, and then the week after, they'll be on our turf. Inside our cage."

"Who fights first?" Nong asks.

"Next week you and Hector. Then Meghan and Jackson the week after."

Nong slaps my hand with a high five.

"You'll see what it's like to fight people who don't know your strengths or your weaknesses, nor do you know anything about them. Well, with one exception."

"What do you mean?" Jackson asks.

"I think Hector may know his opponent."

"Who is that?" I ask.

Mr. Hodge pauses and then says, "Eddie Garcia."

CHAPTER 7

"Do you want to go out to dinner?" Mom asks as we drive home from Saturday night Mass. Despite everything that's gone on in our family, I never miss Mass with Mom. Ever since Dad left, I pray before we go in that he'll be either in a church pew asking for forgiveness or in a chair in the activity hall where I saw that a Spanish-language AA group meets at 7:30.

"Sorry, Mom, I can't. I'm going over to Shawn's to watch a UFC pay-per-view."

Mom looks disappointed. Maybe I should feel guilty, but I don't. I actually feel more guilty spending time with her, like that's betraying Dad. I'd like to live with him. Maybe I could get him to change. But Mom needs me, and I don't even know where he is. She works two jobs. I still work at the garage to help pay for my training, but I feel guilty there too since Dad's not there anymore. It's like he's a ghost every place I go.

"Have you filled out those scholarship applications yet?"

"Mom, I told you, I'm not going to college. I'm going to train full-time for MMA after I graduate," I say. I'd drop out now, except that would disappoint both my parents too much.

"You can't make a living doing that," she reminds me for the hundredth time.

"But it's what makes me feel alive."

She shakes her head. "Hector, that's the saddest thing I ever heard."

"You telling me that you kicked Dad out was the saddest thing I'd ever heard."

Mom looks at me sharply and then turns back to the road. Her jaw is set. "I had no choice. He wouldn't choose his family," she says.

"I wanted him to be a husband. I needed him to be a man."

"He is a man."

"No, Hector. Just being a male doesn't mean you're a man. Being a man means a lot more. It means putting your family first. It means making hard choices and sacrifices."

"How can you say that about Dad?" I ask. Mom stares straight ahead, her lips tight. She's done talking. For the first time in a long time, I think about calling Eddie. He could tell me what it feels like to be an orphan. While his parents died, mine are slowly slipping away.

❦ ❦ ❦ ❦ ❦

"Hang on!" Nong shouts at the TV. A bunch of us from the dojo are at Shawn's house watching an episode of *Fight School* before the UFC pay-per-view. It's a reality show about people training to be MMA fighters. Nong's excited about the one Asian guy on the show, but his guy is on the bottom getting pounded by a mean-looking white dude with a red Mohawk.

"He should grab an arm," Jackson says before he sucks down a protein shake.

"Kimura?" I ask. It's probably the most painful MMA submission, a real muscle shredder.

"That's named after a real person, you know," Shawn adds.

"One day, they'll name a move after me!" Nong says. He breathes a sigh of relief as his fighter manages to escape the second round. It's a three-round fight, and by my count, it's even. Like in so many fights, the third round will be decisive.

"The Nong Vang fly and flop," Jackson says as he pats Nong on the back. "Like how you'll fly across the room and then flop on the mat when I hit you with my fists."

"In your dreams."

Jackson laughs. "It's like that great Pride fighter Cro Cop said, 'Right leg, hospital; left leg, cemetery.' Same with these." Jackson kisses his fists.

"No, it will be the Nong knee knocker." Nong leaps up and throws a straight kick. Nong believes if you take out a man's knees, you take away his power. If you take away his power, you take away the threat. It's good in theory but rarely works in reality. Maybe if Nong would practice more and screw around less, he'd perfect his technique. Sometimes I wonder why Mr. Hodge puts up with Nong's nonsense. Then again, we've all given Mr. Hodge plenty of challenges.

"Just wait until we spar with those guys. I'll show all of you I'm ready." Nong sits back down. "Then, I'll get on *Fight Night* and be in the UFC while you guys are here jumping rope."

"We'll see, we'll see," Jackson says. He cracks a smile, but he doesn't crack me. I'm not thinking about the UFC; I'm thinking about Eddie. I guess I'm happy for him that he must have lost weight to get down to my weight level. I wonder if he did that on purpose.

"So, who do you think gets the W?" Shawn asks. "I think Stan's showing more."

"No way, you watch. My man Kelven will prevail," Nong says.

The fighters tap gloves to start round 3. Kelven is quicker, but Stan's stronger. Like every fight, it comes down to who is smarter. Not in brainpower but in training your reflexes. On the mat, you're not a person. You're an instinct-fueled machine.

Stan scores another takedown, but he looks gassed. He's on top, throwing elbows and short punches. Kelven is fighting them off. Then he snatches Stan's left arm with his right, pushes his hips out, gets his other arm over Stan's shoulder, and locks his grip. Stan's arm is at a painful angle behind his own body. A Kimura submission.

"I told you," Jackson says.

Stan fights the pain, but it's too much. He taps Kelven's leg. Nong cheers like he'd just won the fight. "That guy's almost as good as me," Nong says.

"We'll see how good we are next week I guess," I mumble. I'm worried about the fight with Eddie. Not that I won't beat him—that I'll hurt him ten times worse than he hurt me.

CHAPTER 8

"Hector, be careful," Mom says as I walk out the door. I've been training for two years and have yet to be hurt seriously, so you'd think she'd let it go. But she says it every time.

I head to the garage and pull out my bike. My legs pump hard and fast as I head to the dojo, like they will tonight in the ring. My cardio is strong, and I feel confident with more submission training recently under my belt. Eddie may have dropped out of Roosevelt High, but tonight, I'm going to take him to school.

In the van on the way to the MMA Academy, Mr. Hodge speaks calmly to Nong and me. Nong's talking more than usual—a sure sign that despite his bravado, he's nervous. I'm cold and steely.

The MMA Academy is a lot nicer than Mr. Hodge's place. They've got way more weights and gym equipment. They've set up a few chairs in front of the ring. While Mr. Hodge talks to a tall guy, probably the dojo owner, I'm keeping an eye out for Eddie. It's been more than a full year since I saw him last, not that I'm keeping track or anything.

"We can warm up over there." Mr. Hodge points to a large curtain, like you'd find in a hospital, in the far corner. Nong and I changed into combat clothes at our dojo. Nong's sister-in-law made him a robe with the words *Ninja Warrior* laced in red. Mr. Hodge looks angry at Nong. He doesn't go for showboating.

Nong starts warming up, throwing kicks and punches into a blocker that Jackson holds. I do the same with Meghan. The blood pumps through me as I smack the pads.

"Nong, you're up first," Mr. Hodge says. Nong, Jackson, and Mr. Hodge head for the ring, but I stay in back with Meghan and Mr. Matsuda, although he's on the phone.

"You scared?" she asks.

"Why should I be?"

"Well, this is kind of like your first real fight, isn't it?" Meghan asks. She's right that this is my first time sparring with someone outside of my gym, but it's not my first fight with Eddie.

"It's just another day at the dojo," I say calmly. I'm dancing on my heels as I pound the pads with rights and lefts, throwing in a straight kick every now and then. My plan is to strike, strike, and then strike some more. It will be hard for Eddie to win with my fists in his face.

On the other side of the curtain, we hear a rumbling. Nong's fight has started. I'd like to see it, but I need to get ready. I need to find my rhythm.

"Well, I'm scared," Meghan says. "I think you're crazy if you're not."

"Then I'm crazy, I guess."

"No, Hector, I've known you almost three years and, for sure, you are not crazy," Meghan says. She laughs and I punch harder. "You're one of the sanest and most serious people I know."

Things get louder outside. "See what happened," I say.

Meghan peers around the curtain. "Nong's on top of the guy, trying to finish him."

"Let me know when it's over."

Less than a minute goes past, when Meghan says with a sigh, "It's over. Nong tapped."

"How?"

"I think Nong gassed and the guy choked him out. He's okay, but I bet he's hurting."

I'm glad MMA is not really a team sport, because then I'd have to act like I was upset, like Meghan seems to be about Nong losing. But I'm not, and it's not just because sometimes I don't like Nong much. It's that his loss means I have to win. I welcome the pressure to win.

"Okay, Hector, you're next!" Mr. Matsuda

shouts. I take a deep breath, say a prayer, and start toward the ring. Meghan's behind me. I glance over and catch sight of Eddie. He's not walking to the ring alone either. My Rosie is right beside him.

CHAPTER 9
ONE YEAR AGO

Rosie slaps me hard across the face. "How could you?"

The slap doesn't hurt, but her tone and her tears do. "What are you talking about?" I say.

"You and that girl from the dojo, Meghan. I know all about it."

"There's nothing to know."

"I trusted you, Hector. I love you and you cheat on me?"

I try to hug her, but she pushes me. We're standing outside of school at our usual meeting place to walk home together. It was a perfect spring day until this dark cloud of lies fell over me.

"Here's your ring!" She takes my class ring hung on a necklace around her neck and throws it at me. It catches me just above the eye.

"Rosie, why are you doing this? This is crazy. I do love you, and I didn't cheat on you."

As I try to hug her again, she starts bouncing her small fists off my chest. My instinct after a year of MMA in training is to fight back, but this isn't a foe, this is my girlfriend. I just let her crash her hands into me.

"Rosie, please stop this. I don't know what you heard or from who, but it's not true," I explain. "Not only would I never cheat on you, but I'd get kicked out of the dojo if I hooked up with Meghan. Mr. Hodge forbids any of the guys from dating any of the girls in the dojo."

"From what I heard, I wouldn't call what the two of you did dating."

"You're wrong. I don't know what else to say."

She pushes me, freeing herself. "That's good, because I never want to see you again."

As Rosie walks away, I know that I'll put the hurt on whoever lied to her. I pull out my phone and start calling people. I'd like to call Meghan directly, *but she's never given me or anybody else I know of her phone number. Nong doesn't answer, but I reach Jackson. He denies it, and I believe him. He doesn't even know Rosie, so how would he tell her? Only one person in the dojo knows both me and Rosie. Eddie. Eddie can tell me who lied about me.*

I call him, but it just rings. I text but get no response. I know Eddie wouldn't tell lies to Rosie, so maybe he said something that she misinterpreted. She can get pretty jealous, something I'm guilty of as well. And Meghan and I have been spending more time together because we're both doing Muay Thai training on Thursday nights. There's been a lot of clinching, but nothing other than that. I like Meghan fine, but I'd never cheat on Rosie.

I try calling Rosie again, but she won't pick up. Instead of heading home, I go straight to the dojo an hour before class. I'm lucky that Mr. Hodge is there and he lets me in. I do my best to hide that something's wrong, and I say I'm fine when he asks. But Mr. Hodge is an expert at reading people's body language.

"You want to talk about it?" he asks.

"No." I strip off my shirt and pick up a pair of

gloves. I start swinging away at the punching bag. I burn off anger with my left hand and hurt with my right. I punch until my hands ache. When I peel off the gloves, there's blood on both sets of knuckles. I'm exhausted as I head into the dressing room. I put a towel over my eyes to block out the light. I wish there was a towel I could put over my mind to block out images of Rosie. Images of the two of us together.

"You training tonight?" I hear Mr. Hodge ask. I shrug and glance at the clock. It's six. I should call home and let my parents know why I missed dinner, but before I do, I try Rosie again. She doesn't answer. When Eddie gets here, I'll ask him what's going on.

Mr. Hodge loans me a gi for training, but my head's not into doing the drills. Nong keeps distracting me. I'm even more distracted by Eddie—or rather Eddie not being here. I thank Mr. Hodge but tell him that I'm not ready to train tonight.

I try both Rosie and Eddie again. Rosie doesn't pick up, while Eddie's phone goes right to voice mail. I wonder if he's sick. He's missed the last few training sessions, which isn't good—he really needs them. While he was an okay high school wrestler, Eddie hasn't picked up the other skills you need for MMA as fast as I have or as fast as the other people we started with a year ago. Every time Eddie and Jackson battle, Eddie loses. Most of the times Eddie and I fight, I win despite weighing thirty pounds less and having a shorter reach. I can tell it's frustrating him. The last time we fought, he didn't touch gloves before or after the fight, not that there was much time in between. I knocked him down with a high kick and got his back. I finished him in seconds by locking my arms around his head and neck in a rear naked choke. I could feel him give up even before I cinched in the hold.

From the dojo, I walk in the rain over to Eddie's house. Eddie's little half brother, Manuel, answers the door and lets me in. I head to Eddie's room and open the door without knocking, like I've done a hundred times. "Hey, bro, why—"

But that's as far as I get before I see Eddie sitting on his bed with my Rosie by his side.

"Hector," Rosie starts, "let me explain—"

But she doesn't finish her sentence either. She's too busy yelling at me to stop punching Eddie in the face.

"Tell her you lied about Meghan!" I shout, but Eddie's not talking. I decide to loosen his jaw with

a hard right. He's trying to defend himself, but I'm dominating.

"So she came to you to cry on your shoulder!" A left connects to his shoulder.

"How long?" I ask over and over again. Each time I ask, I connect fist to face until his nose breaks and blood shoots like a gusher. "Hector. If you love me, you'll stop!" Rosie shouts. I'm still punching Eddie when his foster mom yells at me from the doorway to stop. His little brother is crying and hanging on to his mom, while Eddie's dad steps in front of me and tells me to leave.

On the mat, Eddie's no match for me. Never was and never will be. Just like our friendship, I guess—never was and never will be. But in this love triangle, he's won and I've been choked out.

CHAPTER 10

"Ready?" Mr. Hodge hands me my mouth protector before I climb into the cage for the first time. I put in the mouth guard, readjust my sparring helmet, and strap on my gloves. We wear MMA gloves, which aren't as padded as boxing gloves. That worries me—it increases the chance that I'll break my hand on Eddie's thick skull.

I know this fight ends with my hand raised in victory, but I don't know how it begins. Will Eddie extend his glove at the start of the fight? If he does, I will respond out of respect for him as a fighter, not as a person. But he's got to do it. He's got to step up and show me a sliver of respect, if not regret. But either way, I'll dominate the rest of the fight.

The MMA Academy master is acting as the ref. He calls us to the center of the cage. I walk over, head down. "Gentlemen, you know the rules. You'll be fighting three two-minute rounds. If there is no winner, I will act as the judge to decide one. Obey my instructions at all times. Protect yourself and have a good fight. Let's make this happen."

I finally lift my head and stare at Eddie. He puts out his right hand, and I touch gloves. He smiles or maybe smirks but my expression never changes. The ref blows a whistle and it's on. There's some noise from the small audience of fighters, but I block it out.

Eddie comes straight at me. He ducks my first punch, shoots his arms under mine, locks his hands, and takes me over with an under-hook. On my back, I see Eddie throw punches that don't connect. I sense he's looking for my arm, so I keep my punches short and quick.

His mount is sloppy, and I quickly scoot off my back. Standing again, I alternate punches and kicks, but Eddie's defense is strong and nothing gets through. He tries another underhook, and we're into the clinch again. Eddie lands a pair of short knees, but I'm controlling the action, just burying knee after knee into his gut. Eddie breaks away and throws a big, sweeping hook that misses and leaves him open. I land a hard, straight left over the top. Then I rush in and bury him in elbows before Eddie puts me in a clinch.

"Hector, takedown, takedown!" Mr. Hodge shouts.

I use an outside leg trip, and now I've got Eddie on his back. He's protecting his head, so I aim for the body. As each punch lands, I hear Eddie's breath. He tries to grab my arm, then my head, trying to work a submission. I fight that off and stand. I can beat him here. Eddie scrambles to his feet, but I greet him with a left-right combination and then rush in with a knee. He's in trouble, so he grabs the clinch. I force his head down as I throw my knees up, but before I can land a solid shot, the whistle blows. Eddie's breathing heavy; I haven't broken a sweat.

Mr. Hodge talks to me between rounds. "You were surprised how aggressive he was, right?" he asks. I nod and then take a sip of water. "It worked for him at first, so expect it. Can you use that against him?" I nod again. Hodge gives a little nod back before round 2 begins.

Just like the first round, Eddie barrels right in, but I fight him off with more punches and leg kicks. I throw a kick toward his knee, but it's tentative. He snatches my left leg and trips me. Before Eddie can get a full mount, I push off and scramble to my feet. Eddie brings the action again, and I clinch him, throwing a few more punches to the body and more knees. Eddie fights off the clinch and throws another hard right that just misses. Before I can counter, he lands a kick in my ribs that I feel all the way down to my toes. Eddie keeps throwing kicks and punches that miss. Then, before he can plant his foot from a missed kick, I dive for his legs. He tries to shoot his legs out behind him in a sprawl, but I have it locked. I lift, turn, and we're headed toward the mat. As I follow through with the takedown, Eddie wraps his right arm around the back of my neck. Even before we hit the mat, he's trying for a guillotine choke. I tuck my chin to avoid it, but he sweeps and takes side control. He keeps trying for the choke. I fight off the submission and manage to get to my feet. I'm standing for just a second before Eddie wraps his arms around my legs, lifts me up, and slams me to the mat with a perfect double leg takedown. He keeps trying to submit me, but he can't hold me down. We stand again, and while he's fighting aggressively, his punches have no snap and his leg kicks are lazy. I let him bring the action and wait for my opening. He misses another big punch, leaving himself open. I destroy him with a hard kick to the side and follow with punches. He tries another takedown, but I avoid it as the whistle blows.

"You won the first round, he probably got the second," Mr. Hodge says during the rest period. "Work the body. You're wearing him out. He's a strong fighter, but you're the better athlete, right?" Hodge wouldn't say that if it weren't true. He doesn't just say those things.

At the start of the last round, I extend my glove, but Eddie ignores it. We circle and Eddie throws a glancing kick without much force. He tries another, but I grab his leg with my right hand, punch with my left, and then trip him to the mat. I land right on top and take full mount. I snap off a few short punches before Eddie stuffs me back into full guard. I fight it off, and then we're back on our feet. There's nothing behind the punches he's throwing, so he tries for a takedown. He's relentless. When he tries a shoulder throw, I grab his head for a guillotine, but he shakes it off. I counter with knees to the body. I'm off balance, and he bullies me to the mat. He's on top but not in control. I scoot on my butt, making him reach. When he tries for another knockout punch, I deflect it and use his aggression against him. I get my right leg behind his neck while my right hand squeezes his arm across him. He's breathing heavy, caught in my triangle choke.

I squeeze my legs together, putting pressure on his neck with all my strength, and then I feel it: his hand tapping on my leg. He submits. The ref taps my shoulder, and for a split second, I consider not letting go. Everyone from my dojo is applauding. They're my only support now. I listen for Rosie's voice, but I don't hear it. Instead, I hear the ref call us to the center.

"Good fight gentlemen, good fight," he says and gives us both a pat on the back. "The winner by submission: Hector Morales."

The ref raises my right hand, and with my left, I take out my mouthpiece so I can do something I haven't done in a long time when thinking about Rosie and Eddie. Smile.

I turn toward Eddie to show him the respect he deserves as a fighter and prove I am a gracious winner. My gloved hand extended, I wait.

Eddie touches my glove and I respond in kind. "Eddie, did you cut weight just so—"

He cuts me off. "You're the better fighter, Hector."

My former best friend doesn't apologize for betraying me, for stealing my girlfriend, or for crushing my spirit. All he had to do was say "I'm sorry," and so much hurt and anger could've washed away. Instead, he tells me something I already know.

My mind is racing as my eyes scan the small crowd. There near the back is my Rosie, his Rosie. So I decide to tell Eddie something he probably already knows as well. "Eddie, I'm not just the better fighter, I'm the better man."

CHAPTER 11

"Hector, you about finished?" Mr. Torrez, the garage manager asks.

"One minute." I raise my arms to tighten the bolts on this boss Mustang. I'm down in the well, hot and sweaty as I change the oil. One day when I'm an MMA champ, a car like this will be mine.

"Let's go. They're lining up."

Last night, my arm was raised in victory as I defeated another fighter in hand-to-hand combat. This morning, it is raised to perform rote tasks at a hot and sweaty job for less than minimum wage. But I shouldn't complain. Mr. Torrez kept me on even after he let my dad go. He liked my work ethic, but I got lucky in that he's also an MMA fan. He pays me only a fourth of what I make in cash, and the rest he sends directly to Mr. Hodge to pay for my training.

"Line 'em up, and I'll knock 'em down," I whisper to myself. Last night was the first of many victories in the ring. Outside the ring, though, it seems all I have is a string of losses.

𝕫 𝕫 𝕫 𝕫 𝕫 𝕫

After work, as I walk toward the dojo, I try to call Dad several times to invite him to church with me and Mom. He's missed the last three Wednesdays, and I wonder if I'll ever see him again. Maybe on my birthday next week, he'll get it together. On that day, I legally become a man in the eyes of the state. Maybe Dad can become one again in the eyes of his son.

On Saturdays, Mr. Hodge runs a full day of adult MMA classes. Normally I work all day Saturday until church, but with my first fight coming up, Mr. Torrez cut my schedule. Then, after I graduate at the end of next month, he said he'd hire me full-time and put me on the books.

Walking into the dojo is such a sensory experience: the smell of the sweat, the sound of smacking flesh, the rough texture of the mats, and the sight of men and women fighting. Fighting not because they're angry but because they want to help each other get better.

I see Nong thinks the same. He's off in the corner drilling with Marcus Robinson. Robinson fights at the smallest weight class—flyweight—but he's dominating Nong just like he dominates the dojo. He's turning pro soon. The night of my first amateur fight is the night of his last. He's got a perfect record.

"Hector, can you come here?" Mr. Hodge asks. "I'm glad you're here. I was about to call you. What are you doing later tonight?"

"After church, same as always—nothing." He laughs because he thinks I'm joking. But since Eddie, I haven't made any friends who could then just stab me in the back. Since Rosie, I haven't been interested in a girlfriend who could break my heart. My world is as small as the cage.

"I need to get you and Nong back into the cage to get you ready for your fights."

"Really?" I'm excited to be in the cage again, but I'm disappointed it will be with Nong. The only way I'll continue to improve is to face better fighters, even if they're not my size.

Mr. Hodge reads my face. "Don't worry, you won't be in the cage against Nong."

"Oh. Who?"

He points toward Marcus. "You won the other night because you fought a sloppy fighter and because of personal issues," Mr. Hodge says. "When you step into that cage in a few weeks those conditions won't exist. You won't need to be good or great; you'll need to be perfect."

"Yes, sir."

"Okay, get changed and I'll put you to work."

"Yes, sir."

As I'm in the locker room changing, Nong walks in. He's dripping in sweat.

"Good workout?" I ask.

"I'm just getting started," Nong says. "You fighting Marcus tonight?"

"Yeah."

"It'll be so much fun to watch myself get humiliated again. I can hardly wait."

"Wasn't it you who said defeat brews the tea of victory?"

Nong laughs. "Well, actually a fortune cookie said that. But let me tell you, Hector, it's bitter tea. I knew this sport was tough physically, but it's the mental part that really gets you."

"Nong, come on. It was just one fight."

"I can't stop thinking about my mistakes."

"Learn from them."

"Yeah." He paused. "I guess I'm afraid that I can't."

I shake my head. "Nong, you're the smartest guy I know." That might be a bit of a stretch, but not much. In school, I've taken the easy route, while Nong manages both MMA training and AP classes. He's Clark Kent at school and Superman at the dojo.

"A smart guy wouldn't get his brains kicked in," Nong counters.

"You lost a fight. It's no big deal."

"Easy for you to say."

"Why?"

"Because you won."

I don't know how to answer that, so I finish changing. I'm just about to close the locker when my cell rings. Dad's ringtone.

"Dad? Are you okay?" I ask. It's the way I say hello to him these days.

"Where are you?" he asks and then coughs.

"At the dojo, why?"

"You want to get dinner tonight after church with your mother?" Another cough.

I curse under my breath. I need to fight Marcus, but I haven't seen Dad in weeks.

"You look like you're bracing for a kick in the face," Nong says.

My eyes are closed, teeth clinched, and fists coiled. I need to decide. In the ring, you don't choose, you let instinct take over. Outside the ring, things are a lot more complicated.

"One second, Dad." I cover the phone and tell Nong my dilemma, one he knows nothing about. His dad drives him to and from every class, and he says his whole family supports him. Whereas nobody believes in me except Dad, who I've lost all faith in this past year.

"Ask him if likes Chinese, get takeout, and bring it here." Nong says. He doesn't know that Mr. Hodge doesn't want Dad back in the dojo. I wonder if that applies if he's sober, so I ask.

"Dad, I'll see you only if you're sober," I say as I coil my fist tighter. "Are you sober?"

The next thing I hear is a dial tone ringing like a siren in my ears.

CHAPTER 12

After church, Mom takes me out for fast food and then drops me back at the dojo. Part of me wanted to see Dad's car in the parking lot, but the other part is so angry at him that I wouldn't want to see him tonight.

"Mr. Hodge?" I yell. The dojo is dark, with only the setting sun lighting it. "Where are you?"

I head over to the small office and turn on the light. Mr. Hodge's desk is perfectly organized, as usual. Lots of his medals and honors hang on the wall. But he's vanished.

"Mr. Hodge?" I shout again.

The lights turn on, and I see Mr. Hodge standing on the far side of the gym. He's not alone. Marcus Robinson stands next to him. Behind them is the cage. It almost glistens.

I quickly change, say a prayer, and head toward the cage. Marcus is waiting. Mr. Hodge hands me my gear. When I put in my mouthpiece, I feel a rush of adrenaline. As I stand across from Marcus, I decide the best I can do is play to my strength and let instinct take over.

"Amateur rules: three three-minute rounds," Mr. Hodge says as he comes into the cage with us. "I'll act as referee. Protect yourself and have a good fight."

Before I can throw one punch, Marcus crashes a left, then a right, and then another left into my head. He probably could take me down anytime, but he's letting me fight my fight.

"Defend yourself, Hector!" Mr. Hodge shouts.

I'm trying to throw, but Marcus is too quick. It's like he's on fast-forward as he circles, throws a jab, then a kick and another jab. Everything he throws connects, and each hurts worse than the one before. He circles me and punches from all sides. He's a black blur of fury.

"Work, Hector, work."

I start throwing, but it's like trying to punch a ghost. The next time he throws, I duck under and lean in. I get him in the clinch and start lifting knees, but they seem to have no effect. He's dirty boxing, and even though he's forty pounds lighter, he powers me against the cage. The cold mesh sends chills down my spine while Marcus sends an uppercut to my chin.

◦ ◦ ◦ ◦ ◦ ◦

"Hector, you okay?" Mr. Hodge asks.

"What?" I mumble.

"An uppercut like that, you'd better defend against, or you'll get the same result."

I shake my head, which is full of cobwebs. I taste a mouth full of blood.

"Your lip got busted." Mr. Hodge hands me a towel. "Let me see your mouth."

I take out the mouthpiece and open up. Mr. Hodge smiles. "Your teeth are all there."

"Sorry," Marcus says, but he says it to Mr. Hodge, not to me.

"Well, the protective headgear isn't perfect," Mr. Hodge says. "Even in amateur MMA fights with bigger gloves and headgear, you can still get knocked out."

"I'll take it easy next time." Marcus says.

"I don't want it easy," I mumble. "I wasn't knocked out. Let's go."

Marcus and Mr. Hodge laugh. "That's the spirit," Marcus says.

"Hector, how do you feel?" Mr. Hodge asks and then starts checking me for signs of a concussion. Mr. Hodge won't let anyone fight who is hurt. He says he's protecting himself, but I know it's more than that. We're not just his fighters. We're more like family. Then again, just because you're family, that doesn't mean you care. Case in point: Victor Morales.

"I'm okay, but I have a question."

"What's that?" Mr. Hodge asks.

"Can we go again?" Mr. Hodge smiles a little. Marcus helps me to my feet as his answer.

We touch gloves and start again. I can't

match his speed or striking. My only chance is to somehow get him to the mat and work a submission. He's not going to be sloppy like Eddie or the other guys in the dojo can be sometimes. He's going to be near perfect. We circle each other, but once again, he's the aggressor bringing the action to me.

I shoot for a takedown, but he sprawls away, pushing me down with his hips and throwing a hard right in the process. I scramble to my feet, but he trips me and we're on the mat. He lands hard shots as I work my way into full guard. I've got control of his body, but he's beating up on my head. I'm deflecting most of the shots, but every one that gets through hurts and drains my energy. On top of me, his body feels like that of a flyweight, but his hands are heavyweight. Gravity is a fighter's friend.

"Work, Hector, work." Mr. Hodge shouts, then claps his hands.

I eat an elbow and try to get up, but I'm pressed against the cage. It's digging into the top of my head while Marcus's elbows slash at my skin. Sweat, or maybe blood, gets in my eye.

"Work, Hector!"

Marcus fights for side control, and when he leaves the mount, it's my only chance. I quickly wrap my right leg behind his neck and move toward him.

"I don't think so." Marcus pulls his neck away, grabs my leg, and starts to crank it.

"Enough," Mr. Hodge says stopping the fight before I either tap or limp for a month.

I'm prone on the mat. I wipe the sweat from my eye. It's mixed with a little blood, but I'm pushing back the tears. Not from pain but from frustration and humiliation.

"Just because something worked in your last fight doesn't mean it will work again," Mr. Hodge says. "You're an athlete, Hector. Use the instincts you've learned through drills."

My first instinct is to flee from this cage and never return, but that's wrong. The first lesson that Dad taught me was to stand and fight like a man. I accept Mr. Hodge's help to get back on my feet.

"I'm ready," I say and touch gloves. This time I don't circle. This time I bring the fight right to Marcus with punches, kicks, and knees. He blocks most of them and returns with strikes of his own. He shoots for a takedown, but rather than sprawling and dragging him down like the book says to do, my instinct takes over and I lift my knee into his face. Marcus is stunned and tumbles toward the mat. I fall on top and get behind him. I've got his back, and for the first time, I'm in control.

CHAPTER 13
SIX MONTHS AGO

"You're out of control, Victor!" Mom screams at Dad. They sent me to my room, but it's not like I can't hear this fight. It's just a replay of all the others. If my mom only has fifteen speeches, my parents only have one fight. It's always about my dad's drinking.

"I don't need your opinion on everything!" Dad shouts in return.

"You need to get help. Go to AA. Do something. Your family would support you."

"I don't need your support or your help. I need to get a job!"

"You need to stop drinking. That's why you lost

your job," Mom reminds Dad. Dad started having problems at work, getting angry all the time about the smallest things. He always drank, but sometime in the last month, it got out of control. He'd miss work, and when he came into work both late and drunk after a few weeks, Mr. Torrez fired him. Dad threatened to hit Mr. Torrez, which earned him a night in jail. For my sake, Mr. Torrez said he wouldn't press charges. He said while I could stay working, Dad wasn't welcome in the garage anymore for any reason.

I felt like Mr. Torrez was making me choose between my dad and my job. I needed them both. But when Dad told me that I had to quit my job at the garage, I knew who was right, and it wasn't him. Dad hasn't spoken to me since then when he's been sober. When he's drunk, like now, he speaks to me—if yelling is considering speaking. I get either silence or shouts; anything in between is gone.

"Victor, your family is worried about you," Mom says. My older sisters are both away at college, so I don't know how much Mom's told them. I haven't mentioned anything to them.

"I don't need their worry. I can take care of this

myself."

"*But we can help you. Your family supports you. We just can't support your behavior.*"

"*You're just like my parents. You don't believe in me. You think I'm a loser.*"

"*Victor, you're not a loser!*"

Dad's voice drops. "*A man without a job is a loser.*"

"*No, but a man who loses his family because he won't quit drinking is not much of a man.*"

"*Are you saying I'm not a man? Is that what you're saying?*"

Mom starts to cry. "*Victor, you're not a man or a husband right now. You're just a drunk.*"

"*I'll show you what kind of man I am!*" Dad shouts way too loud and angrily. I open my door and run into the other room, where Dad stands in front of Mom. His right hand is a cocked fist.

"*Stay out of this, Hector!*" Dad shouts. "*This is between me and your mother.*"

I'm frozen, unsure what to do. This is new. My parents argue all the time lately, but I've never seen Dad threaten Mom with violence. Mom's eyes are squeezed as tight as Dad's fist.

"*Just go, Victor. Leave us alone,*" *Mom says through tears. Dad looks at me.*

"*Dad, you need to leave.*"

Dad steps toward me and puts his hands up in a boxing stance. "*You going to make me?*"

I look at Mom, then back at Dad.

"*You think you can take me, big fighter boy?*" *Dad shouts. He's moving his hands in the air like he's ready to fight.* "*I used to be a champ. I used to be somebody, you know.*"

"*I know. You used to be my father.*" *His eyes flare and he takes one step closer.*

"*Dad, don't make me do this,*" *I say as I assume my fighting stance.* "*Dad, I'm younger, faster, and stronger than you. You're drunk and I'm sober. How do you think this ends?*"

Dad stares at me, then back at Mom, and walks out the front door without saying a word.

CHAPTER 14

"Some party, huh?" Nong says as he joins me in the bathroom of the Pizza Hut.

"I guess," I say as I finish washing my hands. I hate parties of all kinds. Parties at school that are just excuses for people to get drunk and be stupid. Parties at home when only one member of your immediate family shows up. And parties at Pizza Hut, like this one.

"Could have been worse. We could be at Chuck E. Cheese's!"

"I never went to one of those."

"You ain't missing nothing, cuz," Nong says.

"We did one for my little cousin. Only good thing is all the video games there. I rocked all of them."

I laugh. "Of course you did."

"Wish I could've rocked Marcus like that," Nong mutters.

I share a little, telling him how I got Marcus in a rear naked choke.

"Did he tap?"

"No, he fought out of it and pretty soon I was on my back again."

"I spent more time looking at the ceiling and mat than his face," Nong jokes. He slaps my back and heads toward the toilet. I head back out to the party.

"We thought you'd fallen in," Meghan says. "And all of my hard work for nothing."

"Thanks for putting this together, Meghan," I say, almost embarrassed.

"If I had my way, everybody would be here and it would a party."

"Would there be streamers too?" Jackson jokes. Except for being a fighter and super secretive, Meghan is a pretty girly girl. Although most girls don't have kicks to the head that can put your lights out.

"No, just the four of us is good. We've been through a lot together," I add.

"Like my pops said about basic training. Going through it binds people together," Jackson says. "When times are tough, you need backup. You need your comrades in arms."

"So how does it feel to be eighteen?" Meghan asks.

"No different except I can vote and fight amateur," I say, then reach for another piece of pizza. I decided to go off my training diet for the party, which is easier since Mr. Hodge isn't here. Meghan invited him, but he said he couldn't make it. I guess because he doesn't want to play favorites.

"At eighteen you can enlist for military service," Jackson says. "I'm ready to go."

"Aren't you nervous? I mean, what if you get sent off to war?" Meghan asks.

"That's what soldiers do; they fight wars. They fight and die for their country."

"I think the only people I'd fight and die for

are my family," Meghan says before she takes a big sip of diet soda. Jackson shakes his head like he feels sad for her.

Nong comes back, and the four of us talk about the same thing we always do: MMA. I look around at the other tables—some people I recognize from school—and wonder what silly things they're talking about. We're talking about foot sweeps and butterfly guard, while at the next table, I bet they're talking about prom dresses and graduation gowns.

"Is everyone having a good time?" Mom says as she walks up. She's alone. I prayed that Dad would be with her—and sober. And everything would be back to normal. That would've been a great birthday gift, but no.

Mom smiles. "I wanted to have one slice, since I'm paying for this." Everybody but me laughs. That's the real reason I didn't want Meghan to invite anyone outside of our "fantastic four." Mom couldn't afford it. Since she and Dad aren't actually divorced, he's not forced to give her any money. Not that he probably has any anyway.

With Mom at the table, we talk about graduation in two weeks instead of the fights Nong and I have in four weeks. Mom still hasn't said if she'll watch my amateur debut.

A few minutes later, my boss, Mr. Torrez, makes a surprise visit. It's nice to see him, although it's odd not seeing him in greasy overalls.

I introduce Mr. Torrez to everyone. Since he likes MMA, he asks lots of questions. He and Nong get into a big debate over the best fighters of all time. Jackson chimes in every now and then. If Shawn was here, we'd be talking MMA history until this place closed.

"Hey, Meghan, can I ask you something?" I say in a low voice. She leans over to me.

"Do you really believe what you said?" She responds with a puzzled look. "You know that the only people you would die for are your family."

"Of course," she says. "Don't you think your family would do anything for you?"

I look at Mom, and I think about Dad, but I can't picture him without the bottle anymore. I just shrug.

I've got to stop my family from falling apart, but I'm not sure how. I need to figure out how to win my first fight before I take that on. For all the training I put in, I still feel helpless when it comes to fixing things at home.

"It's all about sacrificing for what you love, you know?" Meghan says. "Look at us. While other kids our age are out having a good time, we're in a gym getting beat up. And we like it. We love the competition."

"Getting that W."

"Well, no, I don't know. If it was just about winning, all of us would've quit that first year when we were just human punching bags. Nong would've quit after getting killed last week. Yeah, we want to win, but it's the thrill of the fight itself. At least, it is for me." She looks up at me. "What is it for you?"

I've trained for three years, but I stumble for an answer. Why am I doing this? Jackson wants to be a Ranger, Nong wants to be a star, and Meghan wants to be the toughest girl on the planet. But what do I want? What am I fighting for?

Mom takes care of the bill and leaves to let us hang out more, but the party is breaking up. Mr. Torrez takes off a few minutes later, never winning his argument with Nong. Jackson and Meghan pour into Nong's Honda, but I wave them off. I need to walk home. I need to answer Meghan's question.

I look at my phone. I haven't gotten a birthday call from Dad yet—maybe I turned it off or somehow missed Dad's calls. But the screen lights up right away. It was on, and it has no missed calls.

As I round the corner to my house, I visualize Dad's truck in the driveway, but it's not there. What is there, however, is a white SUV that I don't recognize. Is it a police car? Is Dad in trouble? I sprint toward the house.

When I get to the SUV, I can't see inside the tinted windows. I knock. The window rolls down, and her words sound as sweet as ever. "Happy birthday, Hector," Rosie says.

CHAPTER 15

"I said happy birthday, Hector," Rosie repeats. Her long black hair and red lips are as beautiful as the last time I saw her. "Did someone make you deaf?"

One thousand words cram into my head, but none escape. I just shake my head no.

"I've wanted to talk with you for so long," she says. When I still don't say anything, she rolls up the window, gets out of the SUV, and walks toward my front porch. I follow her.

When I find words, they come out sounding angry. "Does Eddie know you're here?"

She drops her head. "Yes, he suggested I come over."

"Why didn't he come too?" We sit on the porch with plenty of distance between us.

"He's already said he's sorry, but now it's my turn."

"Not exactly," I spit. Rosie waits. "Besides, you're late. A year too late."

"I couldn't face you," Rosie says. "You don't know what it was like." She still can't look at me; instead, she's studying the grains of the wood porch.

"What what was like?"

She bites her bottom lip. "To be caught in the middle of something."

I show no emotion and no agreement. I just turn and look at my door. My broken home.

"Look, I don't know how things happened with Eddie. They just did," Rosie starts. "I loved you, but I never saw you. You were so busy all the time."

"So was Eddie."

"But he found time for me," Rosie says. "That's how it started. I'd call him to find out about you since you'd never tell me. And then he told me a story about you and Meghan."

"I never cheated on you!" I explode. "He lied if—"

"He didn't say you did, but . . . I don't know, somehow things got away from me." Her voice cracks. "I got to thinking, what if you did cheat on me? What if you did leave me for someone else? What if you betrayed me?" Tears are rolling down Rosie's cheeks. I'm as silent as steel.

"So, I guess I cried on Eddie's shoulder, and somehow, well, things changed."

"They sure did."

"What's that thing they always tell you before you spar, protect yourself?"

I nod.

"That's what I was doing," she continues. "If I broke up with you first, then you couldn't hurt me." She catches my expression. "I know, stupid."

More silence from me. More tears from her.

"Eddie knew it was wrong, and so did I, but it just happened. We wanted to tell you. We just didn't know how. I mean, how do you tell someone that you're breaking their heart?"

"That's what a man would do. That's what Eddie should've done."

Rosie dabs her face with her sleeves. "He told me what you said after the fight, how you're a better man," Rosie says. "You can't just say something like that, Hector. You need to prove it."

"Prove what?"

"That you're a better man. A good man forgives and holds no hatred in his heart. So can you forgive me for what I did? Can you forgive Eddie?"

I am the cage; I am hard and cold and unforgiving. "I can't."

"Hector, come on."

Does she really expect me to just let it go? After what they put me through?

Rosie sniffs. "Is there anything I could do or say that would make you change your mind?"

"No."

She shakes her head, then starts toward her SUV. As she opens the door, she turns around. "Until you forgive me, you won't be free of this.

Your anger is just another cage." She climbs in and starts the car.

I look up for answers, but the sky gives back only darkness. I'm still staring at the vacant sky when Rosie backs out of the driveway and roars back out of my life.

CHAPTER 16

"Hector, I'm praying for your safe return tonight." Mom says as she hugs me good-bye. Then she crosses herself. "I can't bear the idea of you getting hurt."

"That won't happen," I assure her. "Tonight will be fun."

"I still don't know how you can consider fighting fun." Mom shakes her head again.

I remember Meghan's words. *It's not the fight; it's the competition.* It's the rush of testing your speed, strength, and strategy, and knowing that the best athlete wins every time.

My phone buzzes, and it's Nong letting me know he's outside to pick me up.

"Mom, you're really not coming? This is my first big fight. It's the most important day of my life. I need you there."

"I'm sorry, Hector. I just can't do it. I'll support you any other way I can, but not this."

She hugs me tight and tells me she loves me. I don't say anything.

Nong and I arrive at the arena hours before the fight, as required. Mr. Hodge and Marcus are waiting for us. Mr. Hodge looks nervous for us.

Mr. Hodge motions for us to follow. We walk by other fighters, but I don't see my opponent. I'll meet him at the weigh-in. I try to talk to Nong while we wait, but he's silent. When he's nervous, he talks too much. When he's scared, he says nothing.

They call for flyweights. Marcus takes off his shirt and hits the scale two pounds under the max. His opponent is also two pounds under but looks a lot lighter. I kind of wish I wasn't fighting so I could watch Marcus put on a clinic against this kid.

The featherweight class gets called next, and Nong walks slowly up to the scale. He drops all his clothes except his briefs. The judge shakes his head. The scale says 148; Nong is over by three pounds. He won't be able to fight tonight. The veins on Mr. Hodge's neck look ready to explode as he grits his teeth. When we weighed in two days ago, both Nong and I were two pounds under. I worked hard since then to drop a few more pounds since speed, not girth, is my game. Nong puts his clothes back on and stares hard at the floor. The judge calls over Mr. Hodge, and they consult. Nong walks back toward the locker room. Marcus looks like he's ready to strangle him.

"Where are you going?" Mr. Hodge asks Nong.

"Back to the locker room," Nong says.

"The locker room is for fighters, and you're not fighting tonight," Mr. Hodge says. "Sit in the hard chairs with the civilians."

Nong slinks away. I think back to the fights

we've watched at Shawn's house. "Mr. Hodge, I've seen on TV how they'll let him weigh in again. Maybe he could sweat it off or do something gross?" I ask.

Mr. Hodge puts his hand on my shoulder. "You're supposed to make weight at the first weigh-in. That's my rule. You break my rules, and you answer for it."

"You don't need to worry about me."

"I know, Hector."

Being disciplined has come easy lately with the fight looming. "How could he be so lazy?" I ask.

"He's not lazy," Mr. Hodge says. "He's scared."

⬛ ⬛ ⬛ ⬛ ⬛

As predicted, I weigh in at 183, two pounds under middleweight limit. Mark Martin, my foe, comes in right at 185. He looks a lot bigger; I'll match his muscle with my speed.

I head back to the locker room. There's plenty of time before my fight, so I grab a seat. Mr. Hodge and Mr. Matsuda sit next to me. "Let's go over the plan of attack," Mr. Matsuda says.

"Overhand left, uppercut right, kicks to the body, and chokes on the mat if it goes to the ground. But if I keep moving, he can't take me down. When he tries takedowns, I answer with strikes."

"And your plan for defense?"

"He's more experienced in the cage. So, first, I won't let him bully me into the cage. If he does, push back with knees. Keep moving. Be aggressive and dominate."

"And on the ground?"

"He's won all his fights by decision, so he might not have a strong submission game. If he gets me on the ground, I'll try to work a submission from underneath like the triangle choke."

"And what if none of that works?"

"Then I let instinct take over and know that the better athlete will win, and that's me."

"With as hard as you've trained, I can't imagine that won't happen." Mr. Hodge pats my back. He always seems to know the right thing to do or say out of instinct. I wish I could be more like him, both inside and outside the ring.

I start jumping rope to loosen up and shake out the butterflies in my stomach. I'm about to hit one hundred reps when my phone rings. It's Dad's ringtone.

"Dad, are you okay?" I ask. I haven't seen him in a month. I don't even know where he lives. I wanted to mail him tickets for the show, but that was impossible. "Where are you?"

"I'm outside."

"Outside the arena?" I ask. "You came to watch me fight?"

"Of course," he answers. From his short answers, I can't tell if he's drunk.

"Dad, are you sober?" There's a long pause. When we do talk, I ask him and he never answers. Then I ask him to go to AA, and he refuses or has excuses.

"Hector, I need to see you before your fight."

I should focus on getting ready, but I do want to see him. "Okay, there's a door that says Fighters' Entrance in the back. I'll meet you there." I don't see Mr. Hodge, which is good because he would not be happy about this distraction. I head to the back door, and there's my father.

He's in a faded jean jacket and a cowboy hat.

I reach to hug him, but he backs away. "I have something for you."

He hands me a shallow cardboard box. I open it. Inside is a gold robe with black lettering that says "Victor 'Macho' Morales."

"Wear it with pride, like I used to." He takes it from me and drapes it over my shoulder.

"Dad, when are you coming home?" I ask. He stares blankly. "There's an AA group that meets on Saturday nights at—"

"Hector, a man handles things himself. I don't need help."

"Dad, remember when I started this training? And Mom hated the idea? You defended me, and you said you knew I wouldn't let you down. Do you remember?"

He nods his head very slowly.

"Do you believe in me?" I ask. "Do you believe I'll win this fight?"

"Of course, Hector. You're the son of a champion."

"Well, since this is amateur, there's no prize or anything. So why don't you give me one?"

He gives me a skeptical look. "Hector, I don't have any money."

"No. If I win, promise me that you'll go to Saturday Mass with me. Not Mom, just me. That's all I want. Can you promise that?"

He stares at the ground again and then mumbles "Sí." Before he walks away, I hug him. After a few seconds, he hugs me back, and I hear him sniffle. He once told me that real men don't cry, so I guess that makes both of us little boys right now.

⬛ ⬛ ⬛ ⬛ ⬛ ⬛

Marcus waited to shower after his fight so he could help warm me up before mine. Not that he needed a shower since he said he barely broke a sweat in his one-minute high kick knockout. All the fights are ending quickly with knockouts or submissions. None have gone to the three judges.

I put in my earbuds, turn on the music, and just for a moment allow myself to dream like Nong says he does. I imagine this is my entrance music. There are thirty thousand people in the arena, not a few hundred. But all that matters is one: my father.

"Hector, it's time," Mr. Hodge says. I hand my phone and buds to Marcus, who stuffs them in his warm-up jacket pocket. Then he helps me with my dad's robe. As I walk to the ring, Mr. Hodge is behind me on my left and Mr. Matsuda is behind me on my right, and I'm the sharp, cold, steely point of this triangle as I head into the cage.

CHAPTER 17
TALE OF THE TAPE FOR FRIDAY NIGHT FIGHTS

	HECTOR MORALES	MARK MARTIN
AGE	18	21
HEIGHT	5'8"	5'11"
REACH	71"	73"
RECORD	0-0	3-3

CHAPTER 18

The bell rings to start the first round. We touch gloves and both take fighting stances. We circle for a few seconds, but I don't want to wait. I throw the first punch, an overhand left that connects but doesn't hurt him. My uppercut is blocked. Before I can throw a kick, he delivers a hard side kick high in my ribs. I press forward, punch after punch, backing him into the cage.

Martin ducks underneath, and he's got me around the waist. Before I can fight it off, he changes levels and puts me on the mat. I keep my hips moving and my hands busy so he can't work into the mount. He's trying to force me into the cage, but I push back and manage to get back to my feet. We're back in the stance, and I'm moving my head as I throw punches to avoid the uppercut. I throw a knee when we go into the clinch, but it gets me off balance and I'm on my back. Again, he tries a mount. I slip it and regain my feet. I press the action, but he keeps backing up. I try for the overhand left. He responds with a high kick that connects solidly, and I'm thrown. My back is on the mat, and he's on top of me. I try to scoot, but I head toward the cage, and now I'm trapped. Mat beneath, cage behind, and his elbows and fists on top.

"Move, Hector, move!" Mr. Hodge yells.

When Martin's head comes close, I lift my leg and try to get it around the back of his neck, but he fights off my triangle choke attempt. As he does, it opens up his face, and my instincts tell me to take advantage of it. From the bottom, I hit three quick jabs that rock him back. We're both on our feet again.

"Ten seconds!"

I fake a punch and try for a takedown. Bad

move—he blocks it and uses my forward momentum to toss me with a shoulder throw. I hit the mat hard again as the bell rings to end the round.

In between rounds, Mr. Hodge reminds me of my game plan and gives his version of a pep talk. "You lost that round, so you've got to win this one. Stop letting him take you down, Hector. Be assertive and dominate." No sugarcoating, but I know he's right.

Martin and I touch gloves again and pick up where we left off. When another one of my lefts lands short, Martin responds with another body kick. When he tries to repeat, I block it with my left and throw a right uppercut. It rocks him. I follow with a kick to his side and an overhand left. He's against the cage as I pummel him with fists, kicks, and knees. I'm a striking machine.

Next, Martin tries to shoot, so I sprawl. He pushes toward me with his legs while I punch. He backs off, circles, and tries to shoot again. Just like with Marcus, I time it perfectly and my knees crash into his chin. He falls back, and I'm on top unloading shot after shot, including a hard elbow just over his right eye. I try again for the elbow, but he grabs my arm.

"Ten seconds!"

I lock my hands together in a viselike grip, which prevents Martin from applying the submission fully. He cranks my arm, but I'm saved by the bell.

"Good round, Hector," Mr. Matsuda says during the break. "He knows you took that one. Win this last round and you win the fight."

"Make him fight your fight!" Mr. Hodge says. "Don't let him choose his way."

I nod. I'm trying to rest up and stay loose for the next round at the same time. One more to go.

The bell rings and we touch gloves. I start circling, but Martin's feet are flat. He gets lucky with a hook on the bridge of my nose. It stings and I feel the blood flow. When he tries the hook again, I use the opening to throw a kick to his right side. Then another. I hear him gasp for breath. Faking a punch to the face, I throw a hard kick to his left side. He fakes a kick and then shoots. I stuff him, clinch his neck, and bring my knees up. When he pushes out the clinch, I greet him with a left overhand, right uppercut, and liver kick combination. I keep moving and striking while he's trying to clinch and work a takedown. He pushes me against the cage, drops down, and lifts and throws me toward the mat. But before he can mount, I sweep him and now I'm on top. I land a hard right between his eyes. That opens up the cut from my elbow more. He covers up so I can't get anything through and can't see a submission opportunity from this angle. I feel he's about to get guard, so I back away and stand back up. When he stands, I ambush him with a liver kick, a right uppercut, and an overhand left. The left rocks him and he hits the mat. I pounce.

"Ten seconds."

I consider a guillotine choke, but his head is tucked with no space to wrap my arm under his chin. Instead, I throw right after right into his side. With every one that connects, I hear him gasp for air. Finally, the bell rings.

I wait for Martin to rise so we can touch gloves and embrace before the decision, but he's still on the mat. His coach and the trainer rush in. I turn toward my corner, but Mr. Hodge and Mr. Matsuda are already in the ring. "One more minute and you would've put him down."

I'm silent as I wipe away the sweat, mixed now with tears. From the first time I walked into the dojo three years ago, I've been waiting for this day. The greatest day—win, lose, or draw.

Martin's trainer and coach help him stand as the announcer reads the decision. "Judge Horton scores it 30–29 for Martin. Judge Northrup scores it 30–29 for Morales. Judge Stanley scores it 30–29 for your winner by split decision: Hector Morales!"

Martin and I touch gloves and embrace. "Good fight, man. You've got great stuff," he says.

"You too." I look him in the eye briefly before glancing over his shoulder.

I look for Dad in the audience. At first, I just hear and see people cheering for me. I taste the sweat and blood running down my face, and I breathe in the smell of the cage. Then I catch his eye—Dad is still clapping with others in the crowd. It's the first time I've seen him smile in a long time. As I go to leave, I touch the cage again. Yes, I am like the cage: hard and cold. But I when I hugged my dad earlier tonight, I answered Meghan's question of what I'm fighting for.

CHAPTER 19

"Mom, I won!" I call Mom after I'm cleaned up and my cut has been treated by the doctor.

"I know," she says.

"Were you there?"

"No, your father called to tell me."

"What did he say?"

"He said he was very proud of you," Mom says. I wonder if she is too. "He also said that he promised if you won, that he'd go to church with us tomorrow night. Is that true?

"Well, Mom, I think it's best if just Dad and I go."

"Oh." She sounds confused. "Why?"

I pause. I've decided what to do, but I can't tell Mom if it doesn't work. "Just trust me."

"You know, Hector, part of me was hoping you'd lose tonight," she says. "Then maybe you'd decide this isn't something you wanted to do with your life. I just don't understand it, Hector." She's quiet for a second. "If only your father wouldn't have taught you how to box—"

I shake my head even though she's not standing there to see how much I disagree. "No, this was something I decided to do. By training me to box, he just gave me the confidence to be good at it." I knew all along that mastering the martial arts that make up MMA are what make you an athlete, but I'm beginning to think it is who you are that makes you a champion. If I want to be a better fighter, I need to be a better person. And that, like my amateur career, starts tonight.

"Gotta go, Mom. I'll be back in a while."

ᴄ ᴄ ᴄ ᴄ ᴄ

Nong is quiet in the car on the ride home, and I

don't blame him. The only conversation is when I give him directions.

"You don't want to go home?"

"Not yet, I need to make a stop." We drive more in silence until I tell him to pull over. The white SUV is parked in the driveway at Eddie Garcia's house.

"Can you wait a few minutes?" I ask Nong, and he nods.

I get out of the car and go to the door. Unlike last time, Eddie's foster father answers.

"Is Eddie home?"

His face shows his surprise. He scratches his chin, like he's thinking of an answer. "Yeah. It's been a long time, Hector."

I shrug. I liked Eddie's family. I miss them too.

"I'd been meaning to call you," he says, almost in a whisper, as he lets me in. "To thank you."

"Thank me?"

"After Eddie lost that fight to you, he told me he was quitting MMA," Eddie's foster dad says through a wide smile. "He's getting his

GED and then going to Missouri Southeast Community."

His dad calls for Eddie, and a few seconds later, Eddie and Rosie emerge from the basement.

"How'd it go tonight?" Eddie asks once his father walks away.

"I won." Eddie breaks out a smile and puts out his hand. I shake it. "Eddie, what I said about being a better man, well . . . that wasn't right."

Rosie is the one who responds. "No, it wasn't," she says.

"Rosie told me what happened, and it's not right what the two of you did to me," I say. They glance at each other, and I sigh like I'd been liver kicked. "But if I'm going to be a better fighter, I need to be a better person. I need to get rid of everything that weighs me down. Like being mad at you two."

"You had every right to be angry, bro," Eddie says and offers me a fist bump as a sign of peace. I take it.

"So, for what it's worth, I forgive you," I say, although I say it only to Eddie. I just can't look

Rosie in the eyes.

Eddie hugs me, and then Rosie follows. "We're both sorry, so sorry," she says.

"And Eddie, I'm sorry for taking it out on you in the ring," I add.

Eddie holds his chin up high. "I would've done the same thing. I deserved it."

"We all do things we regret," I say. Eddie nods. I hold out a fist as my good-bye, and Eddie's fist meets it. I catch a smile from Rosie as I turn to leave.

ᴄ ᴄ ᴄ ᴄ ᴄ ᴄ

The lights are on in the house, which means Mom is still awake.

"Are you hurt?" are her first words after I'm in the door. She's hurrying toward me from the couch.

"Just a small cut, but you should see the other guy!" I say.

"Let me see it," she says. I push my hair out of the way, and she takes off the bandage. "Did they have a doctor look at this?" I nod, but Mom's shaking her head in disgust.

"Hector, I wish you could know how this hurts me," she says. "I wish somehow you could stand in my shoes and know what it feels like to see someone you love hurt."

"But I'm doing what I love and what I'm good at. You should be proud of me."

Mom sighs and looks me straight in the eye. "Just because I'm afraid for you doesn't mean I'm not proud of you," she says.

CHAPTER 20

After work on Saturday, I have some time before Dad picks me up, so I head to the dojo. Nong's nowhere to be seen, but both Meghan and Jackson are sparring with adults in the Saturday night class. I ask Mr. Hodge if I can join in, but he declines.

"I don't want a day off to celebrate," I say.

"Hector, that has nothing to do with it," he explains. "A fight like that can drain you mentally, and that's when you're most likely to get hurt. You can watch, but no sparring."

"What's going to happen to Nong?" I ask.

"I haven't decided yet. What do you think his punishment should be?"

"I think he's already been punished enough by not being allowed to fight."

Mr. Hodge shakes his head. "Maybe I'll give him a choice. Make weight for his next fight, or I'll ask him to leave the dojo. Does that seem fair to you?"

"That seems pretty harsh."

"Nong needs to stand up and face his fear," Mr. Hodge says. "There's no point in training if he runs away from every fight by not making weight."

His words sound right, as usual. They also sound familiar—like something my dad once told me. My mind digs through memories as I watch the students sparring.

⬛ ⬛ ⬛ ⬛ ⬛ ⬛

"I thought Saturday Mass was at five," Dad says when he picks me up outside the dojo just before seven. I climb in his truck without looking at him so I don't have to lie to his face.

"They switched it." I quickly change the

subject. "I might fight again soon."

"You've got the itch for victory now." He laughs and I join in. He seems in a good mood—and sober.

"Can I wear your robe again?"

"Sure thing, son," he answers. He sounds proud when he says "son."

We pull into the church parking lot after a few minutes. "Not many people here tonight," Dad says. There are about ten vehicles. "I wonder what's up."

I don't answer. Instead, I get out of the truck quickly so I can get a few steps in front of him.

"Did you make some sort of promise to God that if he let you win the fight, you'd take your father to church?" Dad laughs when he says it.

"I didn't need God," I tent my hands in prayer but then turn them into fists. "I had these devil twins. And I had you training me all those years. Do you remember when we started?"

Dad is quiet for a second as he gets out and shuts the truck door. "No, I don't remember so good anymore."

"I remember something you said to me," I say as I walk slowly toward the activity center rather than the sanctuary. Dad follows me. "You said, 'You can't run away from a problem, you need to stand your ground and not be afraid.' Do you remember that?"

Dad looks like he's thinking hard. "No, but it sounds like something I'd say."

"Do you still believe that?" I ask, and he stops in his tracks when he sees where we are.

"What's going on?" But before I can answer, he sees the list of events occurring in the church activity center tonight. There is only one: 7:30 P.M. ALCOHÓLICOS ANÓNIMOS.

He looks at his watch, then back at me. A young Latino man passes by us.

"What is this, Hector?" I hear the fury in his voice.

"When you told me I could train, you said 'don't let me down,' and I didn't. I kept my promise. Now you need to keep yours. If you can't do that, then I don't want to see you again."

"Hector, I said I'd go to church with you, not this. Not this."

"That's not the promise I mean," I say holding back tears. "You also said you'd never let me down. You need to do this for me. And for mom, for Angelina, for Eva, and for yourself."

He stares but says nothing, and I wonder if he'll actually choose to lose us. Then he sighs slowly and takes a first step into the meeting room and back into my life.

CHAPTER 21
EIGHT YEARS AGO

"Son, you know we never want you to start a fight."

"I know."

"But if someone starts one and won't give it up, I want you to know how to fight. You can't run away from your problems. You need to stand your ground and not be afraid. OK?"

"Yes," I answer.

He starts to say more, but Mom yells from upstairs. "Victor, what are you two doing down there?"

"Nothing, just talking," Dad says and then makes a motion for me to be silent.

"Dinner's in a half hour. You need to pick up the

girls from their honor society meeting."

"I will." Dad's showing me how to lace up boxing gloves and telling me stories from when he started boxing at my age. Eventually, he became a Golden Gloves champion.

"Did you box on TV?" I ask.

"No, Golden Gloves wasn't like that," Dad says. "You fight for pride. You fight to prove your skills. And I guess, even though you're a boy, you fight to prove you're a man."

"What do you mean?" I ask.

"They call boxing the sweet science, but it's more than that," Dad says. "Boxing teaches you everything you need to know about life. You get hit, and you get up again."

"And you're going to show me?"

"For now, we'll keep it a secret from your mother. I can count on you, right, Hector?"

"Don't worry, Dad, I won't let you down."

Dad gives me this strange look and it's weird, after talking about being a man, to see his eyes get a little watery. "I won't let you down either."

I hug him tight, and then we finish putting on the gloves. "You're a fighter now, Hector!"

APPENDIX
MMA TERMS

Brazilian jiu-jitsu (BJJ): a martial art that focus on grappling, in particular fighting on the ground; also called Gracie jiu-jitsu

choke: any hold used by a fighter around an opponent's throat with the goal of submission. A blood choke cuts off the supply of blood to the brain, while an air choke restricts oxygen. Types of choke holds include rear naked (applied from behind), guillotine (applied from in front), and triangle (applied from the ground).

dojo: a Japanese term meaning "place of the way," once used for temples but more commonly used for gyms or schools where martial arts are taught

guard: a position on the mat where the fighter on his back uses his body to guard against his opponent's offensive moves by controlling his foe's body

jiu-jitsu: Japanese-based martial art that uses no weapons and focuses less on strikes and more on grappling

Kimura: a judo submission hold. Its technical name is ude-garami, but it is usually referred to by the name of its inventor, Japanese judo master Masahiko Kimura.

mount: a dominant position where one fighter is on the ground and the other is on top

Muay Thai: a martial art from Thailand using striking and clinches. It is often referred to as the art of eight limbs for its use of right and left knees, fists, elbows, and feet.

shoot: in amateur wrestling, to attempt to take an opponent down

sprawl: a strategy to avoid takedowns by shooting the legs back or moving away from a foe

submission: any hold used to end a fight when one fighter surrenders (taps out) because the hold causes pain or risk of injury

takedown: an offensive move to take an opponent to the mat. Takedowns include single leg, double leg, and underhooks.

tap: the motion a fighter uses to show he or she is surrendering. A fighter can tap either the mat or his opponent with his hand.

TKO: technical knockout. A fighter who is not knocked out but can no longer defend himself is "technically" knocked out, and the referee will stop the fight.

UFC: Ultimate Fighting Championship, the largest, most successful mixed martial arts promotion in the world since its beginning in 1993

MMA WEIGHT CLASSES

Flyweight	under 125.9 pounds
Bantamweight	126–134.9 pounds
Featherweight	135–144.9 pounds
Lightweight	145–154.9 pounds
Welterweight	155–169.9 pounds
Middleweight	170–184.9 pounds
Light Heavyweight	185–204.9 pounds
Heavyweight	204–264.9 pounds
Super Heavyweight	over 265 pounds

WELCOME TO

THE DOJO

LEARN TO FIGHT,
LEARN TO LIVE,
AND LEARN
TO FIGHT
FOR YOUR
LIFE.